Acknowledgments

This book is for Zeke, Razzle and Isaiah, true pursuers of bugs and all things adventurous. Hunt on! - RLD

I dedicate this book to my beautiful wife who has supported me from the beginning. - DS

Love and a big fat thank you to Clint, the man of my dreams, for pushing me forward at all times. Zoë, Zeke, and Mercy thanks for letting me give myself to this project. If I could have asked for any children in the world to be mine, I would choose you three every time. Heartfelt thanks to Ben Pasley of The Empowerment House for your kind fathering in not only this book but in life in general. Alberta Adkins thanks for all the great chats while our boys bug hunted. You are one in a million. Finally appreciation is due to Mary Ritchie, Darren Thornberry of Red Letter Editing and Stefanie Rohman for coming along side this writer perhaps best known for grammar and spelling mistakes. - Rebecca

Credits

Find this book online for free on many open source book platforms. Why? Because we want everyone to read it. Find it online in every ebook format for digital readers at www. bookshooter.com—where the independent author can finally go digital! This book was created via a partnership with TheEmpowermentHouse.com—a coaching service for the author who wants to be profitably independent.

Published by Awen House Publishing
Colorado Springs, Colorado
www.rebeccadunning.com

Illustrated by: Devin Smith
Layout Design: Ben Pasley

Printed in the Unites States of America
ISBN: 978-0-9826670-0-2
Library of Congress Number: 2010902551

Beetle Hunter

My name is Zeke and I love bugs. I like spiders! I like centipedes! I like ants! I like big bugs, small bugs, striped bugs and spotted bugs. But most of all, I like BEETLES!! I'm the bestest beetle hunter on the whole block. Today my friends Razzel and Isaiah are coming over and we're going to catch my favorite bug of all … the TIGER BEETLE.

I want to start hunting right now, but the President for the 'Anti Bug Hunting Club,' also known as M.O.M, says I have to get dressed and eat first.

Maybe mom was right. I probably do need some food to make my muscles really big and strong. It will give me something to do while I wait for my buddies to get here. Man, I can hardly wait!

Yes! They're here! They're here!
The troops have arrived. I hope they're ready.
I'll need all the help I can get.

OHHHH! Is that it? Nope.
It's just some ants. Not bad,
but not what we came for.
Hmmm ... these prisoners
could be quite useful.

Ants can lift 20 times
their own body weight,
and they have about
250,000 brain
cells.

Man, this stinks! Just when we were having fun. There has to be a way out of here.

The Goliath "Bird Eater" Tarantula can get as large as a dinner plate and can grab a bird right out of its nest.

Awesome! Look at this. Not a tiger beetle, but not a bad catch.

Check this out! Have you ever seen a worm this big? It would take a huge bird to eat this thing.

There are approximately 2,700 kinds of earthworms on the planet, and more than 1 million can be on just one acre of land.

I don't think we're ever going to find it. We're too hungry and thirsty to go on. We might as well give up.

Yes – food! Saved just in time. We almost starved to death! I must say, rattlesnake sandwiches are my favorite.

Yes! Finally, our prize! The tiger beetle! We've found it at last. The victory is ours!

I'm way too excited to sleep. Tomorrow
we have even bigger plans ... we're
going to track the TUNNELING
CENTIPEDE. It's so ... zzzzzzzz ...

The End

Rebecca Dunning lives in beautiful Colorado Springs, Colorado with her husband Clint, son Ezekiel and daughters Zoë and Mercy. She not only loves to read and write but also enjoys hiking, climbing mountains 14,000 feet or higher, traveling the world and about anything else out-of-doors. Rebecca is the author of two childrens' books: The Real-Life Princess and Beetle Hunter. You can visit her at www.rebeccadunning.com.

Devin Smith grew up in the ostentatious and creative Seattle culture. As an artist, he creates using different mediums and loves to consistently push the boundaries to discover new possibilities. Devin resides in Colorado at the base of the Rocky Mountains with his wonderful wife, Becca. Since "dinosaur trapping..." and being "Super Man" were only fictional careers, his true dream of living the life of an artist from an early age has now been actualized in illustrating children's books. You can find Devin at www.artisanink.tv.